Foreword

The behaviour and adventures of the characters in this book are modelled on those of certain actual meerkats still living in the Kalahari. These creatures wish to remain anonymous to protect their privacy. For this reason, their names and their language have been changed. Any similarity between these characters and any meerkat-stars of stage or screen is purely coincidental. Furthermore, any resemblance between Oolooks or Whevubins on safari, actual Click-clicks or Sir David Attenborough is purely in the eye of the beholder.

Ian Whybrow

Merry Meerkat Madness

First published in Great Britain by HarperCollins *Children's Books* 2012
HarperCollins *Children's Books* is a division of HarperCollins*Publishers* Ltd,
77-85 Fulham Palace Road, Hammersmith, London W6 8JB

Visit us on the web at
www.harpercollins.co.uk

1

MERRY MEERKAT MADNESS
Text copyright © Ian Whybrow 2012
Illustrations copyright © Sam Hearn 2012

Ian Whybrow asserts the moral right to be identified as the author of this work.

ISBN 978-0-00-794115-5

Printed and bound in England by
Clays Ltd, St Ives plc

Merry Meerkat Madness

IAN WHYBROW

Illustrated by Sam Hearn

HarperCollins *Children's Books*

Also available by Ian Whybrow

Meerkat Madness

More Meerkat Madness

Meerkat Madness Flying High

Little Wolf's Book of Badness

Little Wolf's Diary of Daring Deeds

For Laura and Sophie Campbell, faithful readers and kind friends to the entire Whybrow mob.

And with thanks to Dr Stuart Sharp of the Department of Zoology at the University of Cambridge and to Matt Gribble, whose knowledge and first-hand experience of life among meerkats has been invaluable. It was they persuaded me that there is such a thing as Christmas in the Kalahari.

Radiant, Uncle Fearless and their kits Zora the Snorer, Bundle,
Quickpaws and Trouble

Families

Fragrant (Uncle Fearless's sister) and her kits Mimi, Skeema and Little Dream, with Broad Shoulders.

Here we go.
Would you mind just
squeezing down a
small tunnel?

That's it –
down.

Whoops! Watch out
for these prickly characters.

Dodge round them. That's it.

We'll have to go a bit deeper...
and along this narrow passage.
Mind your eyes and tuck your ears in.

Sorry, but this is
the only way if you
want to go where
you-know-who
are sleeping.

Worn out, they are,
worn out but safe
and warm
and well fed...
here beneath the
chilly Kalahari sands
just before the dawn
of a very special
Christmas Eve.

And who snores here,
safe and happy in the
grandest of the five whiffy
sleeping-chambers
of this splendiferous
new burrow?

One more
bend and
we'll see.

At last…!
The royal apartment!

Allow me to introduce the
mighty Fearless, one-eyed
warrior and king of the
Really Mad Mob. Poor
chap, he's done in. Flat out.

Here's why. A flea-hop along the passage and
we come to Nursery One.
Fearless's wife, Queen Radiant, sleeps here,
with her babies...
Zora the Snorer, Bundle, Quickpaws
...Oh, and Trouble.
Radiant's half asleep, half awake, always
alert, always sunny. She takes her duties as
Fearless's queen and soul mate very seriously
and never complains. And her duty at present
is to guard and feed their restless new babies.
Hard work they are, like all babies, but nothing's
too tricky for Radiant.

In the guest room next door to Nursery
One sleeps Broad Shoulders, dreaming of
running his own mob one day. He's got his
strong digging-arms round Fearless's long-lost
sister, Princess Fragrant. Not long ago, they
were outcasts. Both were driven from their
burrows. For many a burning suntime and
many a perilous darktime they were forced
to wander the Upworld alone. Then they
met and their lonely time was over. Safe now
at last under Fearless's care and protection,
Fragrant and Broad Shoulders are expecting
new babies of their own. By the look of her
bump they won't have long to wait. And
Nursery Two is ready, look…
clean-swept and lined with grasses.
Fragrant already has three young kits, though
she hardly knew their father. He was a passing
prince from a far-distant meerkat mob. That
is sometimes the meerkat way.

And here they are,
those hero-kits,
tucked up tight
together in their
own bed-chamber: Skeema,
                Mimi
                    and Little Dream.

They know nothing of Christmas. That's how it
is, as a rule, with meerkats. But these particular,
remarkable kits, were just about to discover what
Christmas is all about.

Chapter 1

Zora, Bundle, Quickpaws and Trouble began it… by being just a bit too good at begging.

It was midsummer in the Kalahari – Feast-time – when there were all sorts of newborn babies and young creatures everywhere.

"Whee! Whee!" said the babies, meaning, *Give us a bite! Give us a bug! Just a little lick! Pleeeeeease!*

Each sweltering suntime brought shockingly big infant animals lolloping and whinnying and snorting and crashing through the thorn bushes. Some of them were happy to nibble the tender shoots and fruits and bright yellow flowers. Others just wanted to chase and pounce. But quite a few of the ones with the sharpest teeth started chasing and nibbling… well, everybody, actually.

"Always stick close to a bolthole, what-what!" ordered Fearless, as his babies squeaked and bounced about. "Remember our motto. *Stay together to stay alive!* And listen out for alarm-calls from the sentry."

The kits had quickly learned how to keep out of harm's way by now. What's more, they were becoming expert hunters themselves.

They dashed among the dunes after the smaller, squirmier newborn creatures that wiggled and hissed and slid. They easily sniffed out the tiny, crawly totterers that waved their legs and feelers or tried to hide from the sun in cool, damp patches of sand.

For a meerkat, a damp patch of ground around Christmas time is like a full larder. You just stick your paw in and grab anything you fancy – lizards, skinks, centipedes, bugs, ants' eggs – and, best of all, scrummy, crunchy and juicy-as-you-like – *scorpions*. Yum!

"They're so *dim*!" complained Mimi to her brothers soon after Warm-up on the morning of Christmas Eve. "They need brains like me, like Mimi!" She often spoke like that – but she was a meerkat princess, remember.

"Who? The bugs or the babies?" said Skeema. He had been hoping to scoff down a pawful of squirming larvae, but Quickpaws came and mewed and rolled on her back. She did it so sweetly that he couldn't refuse her. He handed them over.

"Both!" moaned Mimi. "The bugs choose the most *obvious* places to hide and the babies can't work out how to catch them."

"Don't you believe it!" laughed Skeema. "The babies are much sharper than us. They get us to do the work for them! Look out, Dreamie! Here comes Trouble!"

Little Dream had got rather hot. He'd been dancing a fat but furious scorpion to a standstill. *Forward-back, forward-back, hup-two-three, forward-back.* Panting like a honey-badger, he snapped off the scorpion's sting. Then *hup!* went the kicking arthropod, high into the air. Little Dream had become an expert at this game and fully expected to catch his breakfast in his mouth and chew it up. But just as he opened his jaws, baby Trouble let out a screech like a steppe-buzzard. Little Dream went stiff with shock and closed his eyes tight. The scorpion bounced off the top of his head – bonk! – and before you could say 'Where's-my-brekky?'

his was halfway down Trouble's naughty little throat.

"Bad luck, Dreamie!" laughed Skeema. "You'll have to start digging all over again!"

At that moment, Radiant trotted over, hearty and cheery as ever. "Oh, you poor, dear kits!" she cried, laughing. "Never a moment's peace with babies, is there? Come along, Trouble! You stay with your mother!" she said with mock-firmness. "You let your cousins forage for themselves, my greedy little warthog!" With that she grabbed the little squeaker by the scruff and carried him off to join his brother and sisters in the shade some distance away.

"Now's your chance to tuck in, you two," called Skeema to Mimi and Little Dream. "I've just had a spotted sand lizard. Yum!" He licked the juice from his lips and then hurried to the top of a Kalahari currant bush. "I can watch all round from here. Get your heads down and start digging!"

Immediately, a shower of sand flew up below him as Little Dream and Mimi dug in and shifted twice their own weight of it in a trice. At once, two scorpions, a frill-neck, several spiders and an assassin bug were kicked out of bed.

"I say! Well done!" cried Skeema. "You're still clear to tuck in! Go for it!"

Hardly had he spoken when the voice of Uncle Fearless suddenly sounded the general alarm. "WUP-WUP! ACTION STATIONS! PUFF-ADDER ON THE PROWL! TAKE COVER!"

Chapter 2

In a split second, the kits were deep down a bolthole. They waited, pricked up their ears, lifted their noses. As soon as they thought the coast was clear, they peeped out. There was no sign or smell of a puff-adder. Instead, they saw a sleek young fork-tailed drongo pecking away, tucking in to the last of the spiders that Little Dream and Mimi had just dug up. The little bird looked at the crestfallen kits and gave them a wink.

"Ta very much!" he called cheekily. "Very tasty!"

"W-where's the snake?" asked Little Dream nervously.

The drongo opened his beak and let out a loud HISSSSS – exactly like a striking puff-adder. Instinct made the meerkats duck for cover again, but soon, very cautiously, they could not resist looking out of the entrance of the bolthole again.

"I did that," said the saucy bird. "That was me! I can copy anybody. Listen…" He threw back his head and in quick succession he chattered like a frightened starling, laughed like a hyena, screamed, "*Huu-eee-oh!*" like a martial eagle and finally shouted,

"*WUP-WUP!*" in a voice exactly like Uncle Fearless's!

"You thief! You robber!" yelled Mimi. She showed her teeth and rushed at him.

"Hoy!" said the drongo, hopping out of the way. "Do you mind? I'm only doing what my mum and dad taught me."

Skeema looked at the little bird with deep admiration. *What a trick!* he was thinking.

Just think how useful it would be to be able to do that! "He's right. Let him be, Mimi," said Skeema. "It's just his nature. What's your name, by the way?" he asked.

"Fledgie's me name; mimicking's me game!" chirped the bird. "Alarm calls are my speciality! Chuck me a few more wrigglers some time and I'll give you a lesson, mate. Uh-oh! There's me mum calling. Sorry, got to flit. See you!" And off he flew to join his parents.

"Brilliant!" cried Skeema.

"It's all right for him!" complained Mimi. "But thanks to him and those greedy babies, *I'm* starving and *I'm* thirsty! So I'm jolly well going for a drink! Goodbye!" With that, she scuttled away in a huff.

"Hang on!" called Little Dream. "It's not safe on your own. We'll come with you." Tails up, he and Skeema fell in behind her at a gallop. They knew exactly where she was going. She was heading for the farm where the Tick-tocks lived. Not that the kits actually thought of it as a farm. They had no idea what a farm was, but being naturally inquisitive they had discovered this place very shortly after the Really Mads moved into their new burrow.

To them, the farm was the strange and thrilling territory of an interesting tribe of Blah-blahs. Other Blah-blahs lived in pointy mounds that flapped in the wind, but these seemed to have built themselves a great white lump of an upside-down burrow,

bigger and harder than a giant termite-heap. There was a round fire-pit in front of the 'burrow' that alarmed the kits. But in spite of their fear of the smoke and flames, they were drawn to the farm by the smell of sweet, fresh water. Meerkats mostly live without needing to drink, by sucking the juice out of their prey. But that doesn't mean that they don't enjoy cooling their tongues and splashing about in water when the weather is particularly hot.

The kits had already come across a fair number of Blah-blahs in their short lives. They were mostly tall, pale, harmless creatures, who sometimes wandered across Really Mad territory on two legs calling *"blah-blah-blah-blah"* to each other. Like meerkats, they came from different tribes. The tribe that the kits knew best, the Click-clicks, often gave them bits of boiled egg and let them stand on their heads. They held strange eye-protectors in front of their faces, and they sometimes went *click-click*.

Sometimes other small mobs of visiting Blah-blahs hurried across the Really Mads' territory, making a lot of noise. There were the Oolooks and the Hurry-ups and the Whevubins, all named by Uncle after the calls they used. They were often very frightened of the local animals and hid from them in their mobile escape tunnels that ran very fast on spinners.

As it happened, the family on the farm were not pale like these creatures; these were Zulu people. The kits knew them as the Tick-tocks because that's how the Zulu language sounded to them, with all its tick-tocking of tongues. Generally, the Tick-tocks were gentle and not threatening, moving about their territory calmly and gracefully on their two legs, though they *did* keep a mobile escape tunnel near their main burrow — a very big and noisy and smoky one that roared *vroom-vroom*!

The kits loved to sneak on to the farm, partly to enjoy the water and partly to test their courage. To reach the water needed nerve and skill, for there were delicious dangers and challenges everywhere.

One was the wire fence stretched round the place, which glittered and whistled in the wind. The clumps of fur and feathers that were caught in it warned them just how nasty it could be. But the wire didn't put Mimi off. "*I'm* not scared one bit!" she had scoffed when she first set eyes on it. "I can just burrow underneath. And look! This is easy-squeezy. Somebody's started digging here already!"

Under she went with her brothers following close behind, passing back the dug-out sand, no problem at all. Even so, to reach the water they still had to get past some strange beasts that they hadn't come across before. These bearded, woolly creatures trampled about everywhere inside the fence.

They had mad eyes and sharp horns, but luckily, as the kits soon discovered, they were harmless. They seemed quite happy just to get their heads down and nibble and bleat, "Baaaa… Baaah!"

There were some hungry-looking fat birds there too, strutting about. Luckily they turned out to be silly, clumsy things. They didn't fly up but scratched in the dirt.

"No danger," the kits whispered to one another. Still, they knew that you had to be careful not to scare them or they would flap and cry, "Perk! Puck-puck-puck!" If that happened, one of the Tick-tocks would think you were a striped polecat and come running out with a stick.

As if that wasn't enough, the kits had to face the turning tree that guarded the water. It whirled its arms wildly and rattled and shook. "Take no notice," said Skeema boldly. "It's only making threat-noises. Just wait till it's looking the other way and we'll sneak past." And indeed, when the wind changed and the windmill was facing away from them, the kits raced to lap the water that came from deep under the sand.

It happened that as the kits were enjoying
a refreshing drink on this particular Christmas
Eve, their attention was suddenly caught by
a movement in front of the farmhouse, near
the fire-pit. The young female Tick-tock
and her infant brother (let's call them Molly

and Ajahn) were jumping up and down and clapping their paws together.

Suddenly the Blah-blah papa came running with a loud cry. He had knocked down a young camel-thorn tree as tall as himself and now he lifted it above his head with his mighty arms and shook it at his cubs. As he did so, the mama appeared from the burrow entrance, with a box of bright, shiny things that sparkled in the sun.

"Quick! They're going to attack!" cried Mimi. "Run!"

"No, wait," whispered Little Dream. "They're not after us. Look!"

With a grunt, the papa stood the tree upright by jamming it into the sand, and with many a *tick* with his tongue, and a *clock* and a *tock*, and with many a shriek of delight, the family gathered round it and did something very strange indeed. They began to make a dress for the tree, which dazzled and danced in the breeze, and to hang strange fruit of all shapes and sizes on it!

When they had finished dressing the tree, the adults went away. But then the kits saw another strange sight. The Blah-blah cubs began building a sort of tower out of sand!

"What is it? A nest for termites?" whispered Skeema.

But no. Gradually it became clear that what they were actually making... was some sort of tall Blah-blah like themselves! They dipped their hands into a bucket and began to smooth his skin with water. They made him eyes out of berries and a long red nose out of a pepper. They wound a scarf round his neck, as long and colourful as a rainbow. Finally they popped a bush-hat on his head.

"Look at that!" breathed Skeema, astonished.
"We'd better go and tell the others about
this!"

Chapter 3

The race back to tell the rest of the Really Mads what they had just seen was won by Little Dream. Mimi and Skeema were so keen to be first with the news that they kept charging into each other and tripping each other up.

"Uncle... Uncle!" panted Little Dream, scattering the babies in all directions as he rushed among them.

"By all the paws that drum in the dust…! What is it, Dreamie?" cried Fearless, twisting his head from side to side to make best use of his one good eye. "Is there a rival mob on the rampage?"

"Tick-tocks!" gasped Little Dream. "Bonkers!"

"Tick-tocks?" repeated Uncle.

"Poor little chap. He's got the jolly old hiccups!" suggested Radiant.

Mimi and Skeema arrived, bickering and rolling over and over.

"Steady! Untangle yourselves!" commanded Uncle. "You're alarming the babies!" He could see now that there was no danger, but he wasn't prepared to put up with a lot of nonsense from kits who ought to know

better. "Now stop this argy-bargy and tell me what's going on, or you'll feel my royal teeth in your tails!"

"Sorry, Uncle Fearless," panted Skeema. "But the Tick-tocks have gone daft."

"You won't *believe* what they've been up to!" gasped Little Dream. "... A tree... wearing sunshine!"

"I beg your pardon? Don't you mean it was wearing leaves?" asked Radiant.

"They knocked over a tree," Mimi explained. "Then they made it wear a beautiful dress like the Blah-blah females wear... only all bright and dazzling!"

"Who did, dear?" asked Radiant.

"The Tick-tocks!" said Skeema. "The Blah-blahs-by-the-water! And they weren't eating leaves *off* the tree; they were hanging bright things *on* it!"

"Well, I never!" said Radiant.

"You've got no business to go wandering over there!" cried Uncle. He tried to sound stern, but he couldn't quite keep the admiration out of his voice. "Why, you might have been pounced on!"

"There was a star on top!" said Little Dream.

"So bright!" said Mimi, her voice full of wonder. "It must have fallen from the sky in the darktime."

"And there was a little Vroom-vroom, smaller than me hanging down from it like a fruit," said Skeema. "And they hung other things on the branches... like... sort of..."

47

Poor Skeema, he couldn't think how to explain a dolly and a whistle and lollipops and a plastic water pistol, so he settled for... "a baby-Blah-blah!"

"A tree in a dress, dear? Growing fruit shaped like a little Vroom-vroom and a baby-Blah-blah? I don't think so," came the soft voice of Fragrant, his mama, bounding up to them. "I think you've been in the sun too long." She raised her voice a little to reassure her anxious mate who was on sentry duty on top of the dune behind them.

Just as she did so there was a stuttering roar and a *vroom-vroom!* from that direction. A moment later, a cloud of red dust floated above the trees.

"Stay put! No danger!" came Broad

Shoulders' instant call. "It's the Tick-tocks' mobile escape tunnel – but it's heading away from us." He kept up a comforting All-clear call while the others remained in the open.

"What do you make of the Blah-blahs strange behaviour, Fearless?" Radiant asked her husband.

"Well, now! Come to think of it. Just one moment…!" cried Uncle Fearless, puffing up his fur and standing tall. "Aha! I have it! Of course! Why didn't I think of it before, by all that fogs my royal brain? Now, did I ever tell you about my early

adventures among the Blah-blahs, long ago in the old days, when I was King of the Sharpeyes?"

"Very often," muttered Skeema quietly to himself.

"Do you mean before your accident, Uncle?" asked Little Dream, who was more polite.

"Harrrumph!" said Uncle, clearing his throat. "Let's not go into that just now." It was painful for him to remember the moment in his prime when he suffered so badly. He had dropped his guard for one moment. That was all it took. The Silent Enemy, the eagle owl, had seized his chance, swooping down, grabbing him in his talons and whooshing him high into the air! That was the terrible time when he had lost his eye, his queen and command of his first mob, the Sharpeyes.

Fearless gave himself a shake-up that made his fur snap with electric sparks. *Pull yourself together, old boy!* he told himself. And then he was in command again.

"Wup-wup! Attention, the Really Mads!" he ordered, dashing about and marking the place as his with some well-aimed and wonderfully whiffy squirts. "The sun is at its height," he announced. "The babies are tired. You kits are hot and need rest. Leave off foraging, everyone. Take your positions in the shade. Make yourself ready for Recovery Time, what-what! I have a tale to tell."

Radiant gave him an adoring look and a lick and gathered the babies under a shrub where they flattened their tummies on to the cool sand. Fearless's sister, Fragrant, took her place in the deep shadow of the driedoring bush that Broad Shoulders had chosen as his sentry post.

Uncle made a sign for the kits to move in close to him under the broad leaves of a patch of tsama melons. It was soothing to roll among the firm, cool fruits and to listen to the bees humming drowsily among the yellow flowers. The kits closed their eyes and stretched out, waiting to hear another one of Uncle's tales about his glory-days.

"As I was saying," he murmured, half whispering, "your strange experience reminds me of something I saw long ago with my very own eyes – when I still had both of them to look with, harrrumph! It was in this

very Season of Plenty." He slapped the side of his head with his paw. "D'you know, I do believe it was on this very same suntime! Or was it the suntime after? No matter! The point is, it was soon after the chief of the Click-clicks first brought his tribe to the land of the Sharpeyes, where I was King and Lord of Far Burrow. They were tall and clumsy, but I soon tamed them, what-what!"

"Hooray!" cried the kits. "Well done, Uncle!"

"Shhh! Not too loud! You'll disturb the babies!" chuckled Fearless. A tick on his belly suddenly did what ticks do. Fearless curled up and nibbled at it furiously... "Mmm-nnnyung, you blighter!" ...and then went on. "I wandered freely among their

flapping pointy mounds. Free as a bee. I had no fear of being trampled, not me, oh no! Fearless by name, and all that! Now, on this particular suntime, they all put on their brightest colours and gathered together for a feast, noisy as hyenas. Then they turned a large bird round and round over a circle of fire and gave each other lumps of it to eat!"

"Was it a martial eagle?" asked Mimi eagerly.

"Or an eagle owl?" asked Skeema, thinking of their worst enemy.

"Serve them right!" Little Dream piped up.

"Hush! Voices down!" said Uncle, who had no idea. "It was one of those, I expect. And then," he continued dramatically, "the Click-clicks danced and sang and they covered the tree with bright lights and with shiny creepers, just as you saw the Tick-tocks do."

"But why do you think Blah-blahs do it?" asked Skeema, always looking for answers.

"I'm coming to that," said Uncle. "Just be patient because I want to tell you about something STONISHING that happened next. In point of fact, it is possibly the most STONISHING thing that any meerkat has ever seen Blah-blahs do."

It is very hard for meerkat kits to be patient, but at least they all did their very best to keep silent. Uncle seemed to take ages clearing his throat, but eventually he went on.

"Now, where was I? Ah, yes! All of a sudden a donkey appeared, dashing over the sand and making a shocking *jing-jing-jing* noise! It was pulling a big, heavy, slidy thing behind it. And do you know what was sitting on that big, heavy, slidy thing, holding a great fat pouch on his back?"

"Don't tease, Uncle! What was it?" clamoured the kits.

Ho! Ho! Ho!

"Well, I'll tell you. It was an *enormously* fat Blah-blah covered in a *huge* red skin with white fur round the edges!"

"Did he come for a fight?" asked Mimi. "Was he from a rival Blah-blah mob, come to take over their burrow?"

"Clever of you, my little princess!" cried Uncle. "Those were my thoughts exactly. I thought: *Good show! We're in for a battle here! Now we shall see some fur fly!* Because, I tell you, this fat Blah-blah had a *whopping* white beard! And he was shouting threat-noises as he came, like this: '*HO! HO! HO!*'"

"And was there a fight?" asked Skeema eagerly.

"Sadly, not at all," said Uncle. "The Click-clicks got very excited and charged towards the stranger when he stopped, but there was no biting or wrestling or scratching."

"Not even spitting?" asked Mimi, disappointed.

"No. Quite the opposite," said Uncle. "As a matter of fact, the red Blah-blah dipped into his pouch and took out some bright-coloured funny-shaped packets, big as bees' nests… and he *gave* one to each of the Click-clicks!"

The kits lay, thoughtfully making scratch-marks on the green skins of the little melons growing around them and wondering, *What was all that about?*

Uncle guessed what they were thinking. "I can only imagine," he mused, "that all Blah-blahs everywhere get like this at this time of the year. You see, during the Season of Plenty there are lots of amorous young males on the prowl. My guess is that the Blah-blahs make themselves fine and flashy-looking, and have a feast and do lots of dancing to be as attractive as possible to mates."

"But what about the fire and the sparkling tree and the funny fruit?" asked Skeema.

"Obviously those are the Blah-blahs' way of marking their territory!" declared Uncle. "I mean, have any of you ever seen a Blah-blah who can manage a good squirt?"

The kits hadn't.

"Well, there you are!" said Uncle triumphantly. "The fire and the tree are their way of warning rivals and enemies!

KEEP OUT!"

"What I don't get is this *giving* thing," said Mimi.

"Nor do I!" admitted Uncle. "I mean to say, your drongos and your baby meerkats are sensible; they beg and steal. But when you come to think of it, your Blah-blahs build their burrows upside down. Maybe they do *everything* upside down! But fancy *giving* to your rivals instead of fighting them – I ask you! How silly can you get?"

"They are *stonishing*!" pondered Little Dream, trying out a fine new word. "Like when the Tick-tock cubs made that sand-Blah-blah. That was *stonishing* too."

Uncle was suddenly up and alert, his nose and whiskers twitching with curiosity. "A *sand-*Blah-blah, did you say, Dreamie?" he exclaimed. "No such thing, surely!"

"It's true! It's true! Come and see for yourself!" said Mimi.

He didn't need a second invitation. "I think I jolly well will!" he agreed. He waved to Radiant and mouthed to her, so as not to wake the babies, "Just popping off to look at something with the kits. Shan't be a jiffy."

Chapter 4

Having made his excuses to Radiant and the others, Uncle raced off with the kits to the farm, full of curiosity.

When the little mob came to the tunnel under the wire, it seemed a lot wider than before. "Take care, now!" urged Uncle, taking a deep sniff. "Look about you, kits!" Gratefully, they raced through into the yard and then made a dash into the shadow of the water-trough under the turning tree.

They gazed across the deserted yard towards the great white-painted burrow. There was no sign of the Tick-tocks, but their birds and woolly animals were in a noisy panic, pressing themselves as close to the furthest fence as possible. Judging by the feathers scattered about, some of the birds had been snatched away. Near the fire-pit there was another sad and messy scene. The once-beautifully-dressed tree had been knocked down and lay filthy and forlorn in the dust. All its sparkling clothing and peculiar fruit were gone. And next to it, where the sand-Blah-blah had stood, there was nothing but a trampled heap of sand, some berries, a red pepper and a torn and tattered scarf.

"Oh, NO!" wailed the kits.

"I don't like the smell of this. A thieving enemy has been here!" growled Uncle. Just then, a *vroom-vroom* noise like distant thunder announced that the family mobile escape tunnel was returning, and was not far away.

"Bolthole! Bolthole!" ordered Uncle. "In line behind me, the Really Mads!"

No sooner had he spoken than exactly the same order in exactly the same voice came from a nearby bush: "*In line behind me, the Really Mads!*"

"A challenge, by all that's up and at 'em!" said Uncle, his fur and whiskers standing to attention. He showed his teeth and began to squirt and make spit noises... *FFFTT! FFFTT!*

At once a challenge came echoing back... *FFFTT! FFFTT!*

The kits started to giggle. "It's all right, Uncle!" laughed Skeema. "I think we've met this warrior before!"

But Uncle's dander was up. "Tell him to come out and fight like a meerkat!" he cried. "I'll take on any challenger and give him a good hiding, you see if I don't!"

"Quick, Mimi and Dreamie, lend me your paws!" whispered Skeema. "Let's see if we can tempt you-know-who to come closer!"

They dug away busily until they turned up a creamy cluster of ants' eggs. "That'll do!" said Skeema. "Now hold out a pawful, everyone."

"Come out, if you think you're kat enough!" called Uncle, going through his moves.

"Here, Fledgie-Fledgie!" called Mimi.

"Snackie time!" called Little Dream.

There was a fluttering and flapping, and out from his hiding place sprang – a sleek little bird.

Uncle froze for a moment and then relaxed and burst out laughing. "A fork-tailed drongo, by all that tricks and teases!" he exclaimed, rolling over and over. "I should have thought of that, what-what!! Oh, I've been had, haven't I? Ha! Ha!"

"Hello, mateys!" chirped Fledgie, cocking a hungry eye at the ants' eggs. "Are them there what I thinks they are? My favourites?"

"You can have the lot," said Skeema craftily. "But only on condition that you tell us what's been going on here."

"Fair enough!" chirped Fledgie. "*Yi-Yi! Yip Yap Yip!*" The sounds from his beak were so much like a pack of jackals that the Really Mads dived for cover at once. "That ought to give you a clue!" Fledgie added.

"I say, you're good!" cried Uncle, dusting himself down. "Jackals, eh? Just as I thought! I caught a whiff of the blighters as we were coming under the wire! How many?"

"Don't ask me, matey," said Fledgie. "Counting's not my thing. As many as you lot, anyway. Crafty bunch too! They waited till the coast was clear and then widened the tunnel you kits had made already. They chased the sheep and nabbed one of the chickens."

"But the jackals weren't really hungry, I guess," Fledgie went on. "They were more interested in the sparkly stuff. They're like crows, jackals are. They love anything bright and shiny."

"So they smashed down the tree and the sand-Blah-blah while they were squabbling over the best bits," sighed Little Dream. "What a rotten thing to do!"

A loud *barp-barp*! announced that the

Vroom-vroom was coming through the gates, so Uncle, the kits and Fledgie scuttled back into their tunnel. It was from there that they heard the horrified cries of the adult Tick-tocks and the sobs of their shocked and disappointed cubs as they saw what the jackals had done. There was something so painful and touching about this scene that the Really Mads found themselves holding back tears.

"So sad," murmured Little Dream. "They should never have run off in their escape tunnel. Those jackals were too clever for them."

"Sad indeed," said Uncle, shaking his head as they made their way out the other side of the tunnel. "Come on, Really Mads, it's time we took ourselves home."

But on the other side of the tunnel, Mimi noticed a rather strange sight in the distance.

"What's that funny shape over there?" she asked, pointing just ahead of them. "It's the same colour as a dune, but it's not a dune. Maybe it's another smashed sand-Blah-blah!"

Uncle strained his one eye to look as they cautiously approached, but it was only when they were quite close that he could make sense of it. "A female ostrich, by all that's long-necked and leggy!" he announced. "They throw themselves flat like that when they're in danger or distress."

And indeed, at that moment, the pile

of sand rearranged itself into an enormous bird that staggered for a moment on her scaly, towering legs. She flapped her wings, moaned and then plumped down on a smooth rock. "Where are you, my chick? Come to me, my chickie! Crrrrroooo. Mummy keep you warm."

"Is she mad?" Mimi asked Uncle. "She's sitting on a stone!"

"Terrified by the jackals, I should say," said Uncle, as the bird staggered to her feet once more and then threw herself flat again.

The *pad-pad-pad* of hurrying footfalls close by sent the Really Mads running for a bolthole and sent Fledgie flip-flapping into the air. But as they soon discovered, they had no need to worry. It was only the young Tick-tocks. They had seen that the female ostrich was in trouble and, forgetting their own misery, had brought a bucket of water to try to revive her.

"Jackals!" screamed the poor deluded creature, springing up. "Get away from us! Biff! Where are you? We need your help!

The jackals are back! They're trying to steal our chickie, Biff!" She began to leap and kick out. "Get back, you nest-robbers!"

The little Zulu children, Molly and Ajahn, heard the commotion and though they understood very well that one blow from those terrible claws could kill them, they bravely moved as close to the distressed bird as they could and set down a bucket of water in front of her. Having done that, they turned and calmly walked at a good steady pace towards the safety of the farmyard. They knew better than to run. They knew that even if they ran twice as fast as the best human sprinter in the world, she could still outrun them.

The water seemed to calm the poor,

confused creature. She turned an enormous eye towards the bucket, sniffed its contents and plunged her head in. Like meerkats, ostriches can go without water for ages, but when they're exhausted there's no better pick-me-up. She drank deep, and a few moments later she stepped back, water dripping from her broad, silvery beak and flipping in all directions from her frantic eyelashes. Strangely, the act of drinking seemed to have used up the last of her strength – or her will to live – and she collapsed into a sand heap once more.

Fledgie fluttered down by her ear and made a low, booming sound, the call of a male ostrich: *Wooo-ooo-OOOoooo!*

The fallen ostrich just about found the strength to open her eye halfway. "Is that you, Biff?" she murmured as if she were in a dream. "You've found your Sprintina at last! Crrrrooo! I thought the cheetahs might have caught you. I knew you wanted them to chase you so that I and the other wives could get away. But I didn't run, Biff! I stayed to cover the eggs. I waited on the nest for you, Biff, waited and waited. I thought you were dead, but here you are! You were too speedy for them, my long-legged love!"

Her voice was getting softer now, harder to hear. Then suddenly she seemed to jerk herself awake. For the first time she became aware of little furry faces gathered round her. "Who are you? Where's Biff? Where's my chickie?" She gave another jerk, as though she was living through her nightmare once more. "The jackals!" she cried. "Ohhh, deep in the darktime, the jackals came! I kicked! But so many of them! Too many! I chased one, then another. That's how they tricked me. Stole all our eggs one by one... Till only one chickie was left... the one who called out to me through his shell... But the jackals ganged up and chased me away. I ran and ran... lost my way... lost my Biff... lost our last chickie..."

Her strength had finally drained away and she fell once again into a deep sleep.

Uncle spoke for all those watching and listening. "So, our old foe the sneaking Black-backs have struck again, by all that yelps and cackles!" he growled bitterly. "The cunning of the brutes! To wait until the cheetahs chase away her mate and the rest of his wives and then to sneak back to steal the eggs from under her, what-what!"

"But she said they stole all the eggs *except one*," said Skeema. "You heard her. *'Till only one chickie was left,'* she said. Maybe it's still in the nest, trying to hatch."

"So unfair!" cried Mimi. "Imagine hearing your baby's voice, and then losing him in the dark!"

"We all know what it's like to lose a mama. We've got to do something!" said Little Dream. "We should go and search for the last of her eggs… or maybe look for her mate, Biff."

"Now, look here," said Uncle. "Let's be sensible. Apart from not knowing where to look, we don't know whether the chick is still in the egg or whether the jackals have eaten it. And even if Biff was fast enough to run away from the cheetahs and not get eaten, we have no idea what he looks like!"

"That's true," admitted Skeema. "But Uncle, look at it this way. If the chickie *is* still alive, he won't live through the darktime cold unless there's someone there to keep him warm. We're his only hope. Don't you think we should at least try to find him?"

Uncle cleared his throat. *Harrrumph.* "Well, now, look here, I don't know which is the deadlier enemy: your cheetah or your jackal. Your cheetah will outrun you and your jackal will outsmart you. Still, I must say those young Tick-tocks got me thinking when they brought water out here to comfort a poor distressed ostrich. They risked a good kicking, you know. I know that's silly, but it's also rather splendid – this *giving* thing they do in the Season of Plenty – don't you agree?"

"Absolutely!" chorused the kits.

"So, here's the thing. Can we honestly call ourselves the Really Mads and not take a few risks for others ourselves?"

"No!" yelled the kits. "No way! Let's go!" and their excited cries were copied exactly by Fledgie. *No way! Let's go!*

"Come along then. Brace yourselves for an adventure, my brave-hearts!" said Uncle, feeling proud to be in charge of them. "We'll start by following these jackal tracks towards the place where the sun drops out of sight in the darktime. Westward, ho!"

"Westward, ho!" cried the others.

Chapter 5

In the heat and in the featureless, foreign territory where few trees cast shadows, the Really Mads had a hard time of it. They all understood the risks they were taking. They all knew that they were wide open to attack every step of the way.

Concentrating on following the trail of the Black-backs meant heads down and noses twitching. That was dangerous. The

Silent Enemy may be dead – the eagle owl that had taken Uncle's eye in that fateful battle long ago – but there were plenty of goshawks and martial eagles circling in the sky that were just as deadly.

"Good thing we've got Fledgie flying overhead, keeping a look-out!" puffed Skeema, galloping on strongly, keen as a small hound.

"Hear, hear!" said Uncle. "Remind me to make him an honorary Really Mad when this is over!" He might have added, 'If we ever get home alive,' but he was too good a leader to say so out loud.

The tracking was made harder because the padprints of the jackals often got trampled by the hoofprints of vast numbers of other creatures that were moving about in search of the greenest grazing, as was the way in the Season of Plenty.

Uncle could feel the ground trembling as hundreds of gemsbok, eland and red hartebeest went pushing along to the east of them, but not near enough to be a danger.

So on they went, dodging among blue pea, driedoring and candle thorn bushes, now and then risking a detour among tall whispering herbs and golden grasses leaping with hares and springbok. "Too tall, too tall!" muttered Uncle, knowing that this prairie was just the sort of territory where cheetahs creep, scheming to get within sprinting distance of anything edible. He raised his

voice and cried, "Boltholes! Boltholes!" to the kits as a warning for them to be ready to get underground at a moment's notice.

But there were no holes in sight when the earth trembled and the grasses parted just in front of them and suddenly they were face to face with a muddy, snorting creature with wild eyes and swept-back piggy ears. It was a male white rhino calf, twenty times their size. When he saw the meerkats he skidded to a halt and squealed with fright.

"A square-lip!" shouted Skeema. "What do we do, Uncle?"

"S-stand together!" cried Little Dream bravely. "Make ourselves big!"

"It's only a baby!" put in Mimi. "He won't hurt us, will he?"

"The baby's not the problem," said Uncle, as his one eye settled on a movement in the grass behind the calf. "It's his mother we need to worry about! RUN FOR YOUR LIVES!"

There was a snarl and a furious shriek and the sound of thunder from somewhere just behind the rhino calf. It was indeed the calf's mama! If she had kept her enormous head down and simply carried on charging, no doubt she could have skewered all four of the Really Mads on her deadly twin horns or, more likely, squished the lot of them like bugs. Luckily she took a moment to display her favourite threat-move. That involved standing still with her great, long head down, snorting and bellowing and then sweeping her horns from side to side along the ground like a scythe.

"Head for those camel thorn trees!" yelled Uncle. "And whatever you do, don't look back!"

The kits didn't need to be told twice. They dashed for the clump of trees like mice with an aardwolf on their tails. They had got as far as a large, blotchy yellow boulder that was lying in their path when, without warning, it decided to stand up. "Jump!" yelled Skeema and the four of them had to spring like gazelles to clear it.

"Sorry, Mister," puffed Little Dream, who was last over. But the leopard tortoise (for that's what the boulder was) was too busy chewing a desert thistle to even notice, let alone demand an apology.

The mother rhino was gathering speed now, nosing her excited baby along as she charged.

Fledgie swooped low over the Really Mads' heads. "Keep going! There's a nice safe hole straight ahead!" he chirruped encouragingly. And sure enough, they saw it – and smelled it – under the tangled roots of the nearest camel thorn tree.

Uh-oh, thought Uncle. *Let's hope the owner of this hole is not at home when we call, what-what!* Though he was wise enough to keep the thought to himself, knowing they'd just have to risk it. "DIVE! DIVE! DIVE!" he shouted, and the Really Mads plunged into the darkness of the den.

"Phew!" gasped the Really Mads as they collapsed in the safety of the bolthole, panting and listening while the rhino took out her temper on the trunk of the tree. It was a while before she lifted her head and trotted proudly away.

As soon as the coast was clear, the kits emerged from the hole.

"What's happened to Fledgie?" asked Little Dream, glancing up at the sky.

"This might attract his attention," said Skeema and he gave his faithful Snap-snap a couple of

SQUEAK!

squeezes. SKWEE-SKWEE!

"Skwee-swee," came an echoing call and very soon the cheery drongo was fluttering down to join them.

"A near thing, what-what!" exclaimed Uncle, snuffling among the scrapes and hollows churned up by the rhinos' pounding hooves. The little mob looked all around in dismay. The Black-backs' trail seemed to have disappeared completely. "Harrumph," said Uncle, looking down into each of the little faces that were raised towards his. "I'd say that our chances of finding Sprintina's chick are now – um – what's the number that comes before number one?"

"Don't ask me," chirped Fledgie. "I told you, I'm rubbish at counting."

"I think it's 'hero'," said Skeema. "Or something like that. What do you think, Dreamie?"

"I don't think it's 'hero', because that's what Uncle is," said Little Dream thoughtfully. "But nothing comes before number one, surely."

"That's the one, Dreamie!" cried Uncle, patting him on the back. "*Nothing!* Well done. That's just the word I was looking for! As I say, we've got just about a *nothing* chance of finding any lost chickie now. So we've got to decide as a team. Do we give up? Or shall we do the mad thing and..."

"...CRACK ON!" exclaimed the kits, holding their chins high, finishing his sentence for him.

"Good show! Just what I hoped you'd say," said Uncle. "I'm proud of you!"

"Skwee-skweeee!"

"Wha…? Who was that? Was that your Snap-snap making me jump, Skeema?"

"No, matey, it was me!" tweeted Fledgie. "If you lot would just let me get a chirp in edgeways, I was going to tell you that I've spotted a big old nest in the sand – down by the riverbed over that rise there!"

"Then what are we waiting for?" yelled Uncle. "Let's crack on!"

Chapter 6

The nest that Fledgie led the Really Mads to was a sorry sight. At its best, it should have been a neat circular pit in the sand with perhaps ten or twenty eggs packed neatly together in it. But this was a shapeless mess. There were hundreds of prints in the scuffed-up sand. Nevertheless, it was still just possible to pick out the wide three-toed marks of ostrich feet, running in all

directions away from the place. Sadly, these were easily outnumbered by the tell-tale four-clawed pawprints and skid-marks and scrapings of jackals in a feeding frenzy.

"All the eggs have gone," murmured Little Dream, gazing sadly at the signs of destruction.

"The jackals have taken the lot," groaned Skeema.

"Well, we rather expected that," said Uncle.

Great soft bunches of giant tail plumes and wing feathers lay all about. Mimi began to nose among them. "So pretty!" she crooned sadly. "So warm and soft!"

"That's the way," said Uncle, giving himself a good shake-up. "Good thinking, Mimi! The least we can do is tidy up a bit. Lend us a paw, everyone."

The meerkats began to scrape the nest back into shape with their long digging-claws. They lifted the loose red sand gently and reverently, because, in a way, they felt they were building a small monument here by an almost dried-out riverbed in a strange and barren land. Meanwhile,

Fledgie swooped about, picking up ostrich-feathers in his beak, gathering them into a heap. It lifted everybody's spirits to be busy, and suddenly there was a cry of surprise and delight from Little Dream. "What is it?" asked the others.

"I thought it was a stone or a pebble or something," said Little Dream, pulling away gently at some loose sand from a heap lying just to the side of the ruined nest. "But then I thought I heard a noise." He carried on brushing and blowing carefully and he very soon laid bare something smooth and white and oval.

The others rushed to help and in no time they uncovered it completely. There it was, in spite of their worst fears: an ostrich egg, as big as the kits themselves!

"Is it warm?" asked Fledgie, hopping about excitedly.

As one, the Really Mads threw their arms round it to feel it.

"A group hug, eh?" chirruped Fledgie. "Well, that's one way to warm it up, I s'pose! Move over so that I can get my ear against the shell too!"

They stood back while he settled himself on the pointy end of the egg and bent forward to press his ear against it. "It's not easy," he muttered. "This shell's really thick. Wait."

The Really Mads held their breath. For a while there was nothing but the usual desert song of rustling cicadas, calling birds and snorting animals.

The waiting got too much for Mimi. "I'm sure *I* can hear something!" she whispered. "Like a *chip-chip* or something."

"You mean a sort of tapping?" breathed Uncle, delighted.

"No, it's a sort of a *cheep*. I can hear it now too," said Skeema. "What do you reckon, Fledgie? Is that a little voice in there?"

"What's it saying?" whispered Mimi urgently. "Tell me, tell Mimi!"

"Give us a chance! Shussshhh!" scolded Fledgie. "Wait. I've got it now. It's a voice. There it is again…"

Now Uncle lost his patience. He was bursting to know. "What's the voice saying, by all that's tense and teasing?" he demanded.

Fledgie pulled himself upright and spoke. "It was ever so faint, but I think it said: 'Mum, *where are you? Too cold.*'"

"Is that all?" gasped Uncle.

"That's it," replied Fledgie. "And now it's gone quiet again."

"It's Sprintina's last chickie! It's got to be! We've found him!" cried Little Dream, hardly able to contain himself.

"Now, now," said Uncle. "Let's not get carried away, Dreamie, lad," said Uncle kindly. "I know it said 'Mum'. And I understand that mother ostriches bond with their chicks by talking to them while they're still inside the shell. So it *might* be Sprintina's chickie, but we don't know for sure, do we?"

"Then we shall jolly well have to take the egg to Sprintina and find out!" cried Skeema, who felt much the same as his brother. The trouble was that, try as he might, he couldn't think up a plan for moving it.

"Far too big and heavy!" sighed Uncle. "Why, the whole mob of us – Fledgie included – could hardly lift it! And it'll be darktime soon. If we don't dash home sharpish, or at least get below ground, we shall all catch our death of cold."

"But if we leave the egg by itself in the open, the chickie will die and never see its mother!" wailed Little Dream.

Instead of talking, Mimi was busy moving the pile of ostrich feathers that Fledgie had collected up. "Now, Mimi! Really!" scolded Uncle. "This is no time for thinking about adding to your fancy headgear! We have a serious problem!"

Mimi was very proud of her headband, and quite rightly. She was the only meerkat princess in the Kalahari to wear a coronet decorated with porcupine quills and the feathers of a secretary-bird. But for once, her mind was not on herself. "Well, the rest of you can go back to the burrow if you like," she said. "Or you can go and spend the darktime in a bolthole somewhere. *I* intend to stay here and keep the chickie warm!"

"It's all very well you warming the chickie," said Uncle, rather tempted to give her a nip for cheek. "But how exactly are you going to keep from freezing?"

"The same way ostriches do!" cried Mimi triumphantly. "By wrapping us all up with feathers!" To demonstrate, she jumped on board the egg and arranged the softest, warmest plumes around her.

"Brilliant!" cried Skeema. "I couldn't have thought of a better idea myself!"

"Good show!" said Uncle. "It's a very clever scheme. But, Mimi, I'm afraid it will take more than plumage and pom-poms to stop this little feller from freezing. If indeed it is a feller. He's going to need all the fur coats we can muster as well! So move over, my dear, and we'll all cuddle up together."

"Me and all?" chirped Fledgie doubtfully, glancing towards the sinking sun.

"No need for that," said Uncle. "But I was thinking," he continued, "ostriches do tend to run round in circles when they get in a flap. It's just possible that Biff is running round in circles not too far away."

"So you want me to go and look for him? No problem! Leave it to me! I've never tried navigating by starlight, but I'll do me best to locate him. I'll find him if I can!" chirped the brave little drongo.

"Bravo!" cried Uncle. "Because if the chickie *does* happen to hatch, he's going to need his papa to teach him the Ostrich Way – how to do pecking and strutting and kicking and such, what-what!"

And so it was, one cold and frosty Christmas Eve in the Kalahari, that a little mob of brave and determined meerkats did their best to protect a stranger's egg and keep it safe and warm. And while they settled down, a little fearfully, to watch and wait, they called goodbye and good luck to an equally brave and determined little fork-tailed drongo.

"See ya later, incubators!" he sang.

He rose into a sky that was lit by stars, one of them *stonishingly* bright.

Chapter 7

"Wh-while m-meerkats watched their nest by starlight…"

Little Dream hummed to himself as he peered up at the star-pricked blackness. He was shivering as he hummed, though not really because of the cold. He felt cold, certainly, mostly on his ears and nose when he popped them up above his ostrich-feather bed. But he was also shivering because he couldn't stop thinking of all the many frightening things that might be lurking close by in the dark. Composing a song helped him keep his mind off them.

He was pleased with his first line and tried to think of another good one. A lion sent up a warning roar. It was so long and low and rumbling that Little Dream imagined the sound filling the nearly-dry riverbed and rolling down it like floodwater. He hurried on with the next line:

"All seated on the sand..."

He didn't much like that one and tried another:

"They hoped the egg might hatch..." That gave him an idea for a way to finish the verse, but just as he was about to compose

the next lines Uncle began to stir.

"Grrr!" growled Uncle suddenly. "Get orf, you blighter!" Try as he might to keep awake, Fearless had fallen asleep for a moment and was now dreaming. Up came his back foot and started knocking against his nose, jerking Mimi and Skeema awake.

"Wazzat?" blurted Skeema. "Is there a raid?" He grasped Snap-snap tighter, ready to make him go *Skwee-skwee*! in the face of any intruder.

Mimi was up on her hind legs in a flash, making spit-noises. "No, no," said Dreamie. "It's just Uncle having one of his bad dreams." Fearless stirred again in his sleep and mumbled the start of his battle-cry:

"Shaky-shaky! Boom-boom! Call!"

Knowing how tired their dear old guardian
must be, the kits did the sensible thing and
sat on his head until he felt warm enough
and safe enough to slip back into a peaceful
sleep once more.

"No raid. All's well," said Little Dream,
trying to sound confident. "I say, I've made

up a song. Would you like me to teach it to you?"

"All right, if you must," said Skeema, stifling a yawn.

"Let's hear it, then," said Mimi sharply. "But cuddle up closer to the egg, both of you. We've got a job to do, remember."

"Yes, yes," agreed Skeema, too worn-out to be bothered to squabble.

So Little Dream cuddled up to the egg and sang the whole verse through for them:

"While meerkats watched their nest by starlight
They hoped the egg might hatch,
A flea came down on Uncle's nose
And he began to scratch."

Mimi and Skeema really liked it. In fact they made up a nice tune for it and sang it over and over until they had learned it by heart. They only stopped because they suddenly realised that something was tapping in time to the music on the shell of the egg! Quickly they pressed their ears to it. "It's coming out! It's hatching!" they gasped. Then they realised that the tapping was on the outside. It was made my Uncle's digging-claw.

"I heard what you just sang, you young dung-beetles," he chuckled, giving them each a playful jab. "Cheeky... but very amusing. All that howling should give the hyenas something to think about, by all that's larky! So, come along, then. While you're in good voice, let's try one of my songs. It goes like this:

"Good King Fearless once walked out
Looking for a chickie;
Soon the sand lay round about
Cold and damp and sticky.
"Sing with me!" said Little Dream.
"It will help the time go -
Till we hear a cheery chirp

*From a daring dro-**ong**-go!*"""

They clung to the egg and sang together at the tops of their voices. They wanted to show the lurking leopards and the caracal cats and the lions and the cheetahs and the foxy foxes – not to mention any cackling jackals who happened to be within earshot – that meerkats were proud and loud and not to be pounced on. Overhead, stars shot across the sky like sparks from a fire and the brightest one, the one to the east, seemed to pulse like a little sun.

"I bet that's shining right over our new burrow," said Uncle.

"And on the water by the Tick-tocks' burrow," added Skeema.

"I bet if we followed that star it would

lead us right back to where Sprintina's lying in a heap," said Mimi. "How I should *love* to be able to take this egg to her."

"Yes, but we should very much like to take it home with *us*," came a soft, sly voice from the darkness of the dry riverbed.

"Step away from the nest and we might not tear you to pieces," said another, this time from the opposite direction.

At once the Really Mads were up and bristling. "WUP-WUP! BATTLE STATIONS! STAND BY TO REPEL BOARDERS!" cried Fearless. "THE BLACK-BACKS ARE HERE!

Chapter 8

Tails up, rocking backwards and forwards, trembling (not with terror but with rage) all the kits joined in the mob war dance and battle-cry.

"*Bouncy-bouncy*
Boom-boom call!
Stand-up! Tail-up!
Make yourself tall!
Head-butt! Head-butt!

Strike like a snake!

Spit-spit-spit-spit!

Shaky-shake-shake!"

They were surrounded by a pack of at least five Black-backs, maybe more. They could tell that just from the power of the stink that came at them from all sides. Not only that, but the sunlight of Christmas morning was *just* beginning to melt the darktime, which meant that the defenders could just make out their slippery black shadows – now slinking closer, now flattening themselves in the cold sand. It was only a matter of time before the jackals closed in for the kill.

The Really Mads knew exactly what to expect from these invaders. One would rush at you, and while you were trying to fight that one off, another would sneak up and attack you from another angle. The meerkats had seen off a jackal-attack before, but on that occasion they had had strong support from a friendly lion-cub and his fearsome mama and aunts. This time, they were on their own and they had very little room for manoeuvre. They couldn't line up and charge. They couldn't run for higher ground. They couldn't retreat down a bolthole. If they made any of these moves, one of the enemy warriors would rush forward and grab the egg they were guarding!

Fearless quickly chose the only battle-plan available. "STAND FIRM AND SHOW 'EM YOUR TEETH!" he roared. And so they did, staring into the gloom, each backed up close against the egg. They puffed out their fur and tried to look as dangerous as they possibly could, running their deadly digging-claws along their teeth to make them rattle.

"SKWEE-SKWEEEEE!" screamed Snapsnap, in a defiant warning.

The time had come, Fearless felt, to rally his troops with a rousing speech. "Never in the history of meerkat conflict," he began, his voice low and steady, "have so many big stinkers been stood up to by so few small heroes. We can expect at any moment now, the fury and might of these shadowy cowards to be unleashed upon us. And for what? For an egg. For a helpless chick. A chick whose little feathers are still wet. A chick unwarmed yet by the sun."

"Stop," came a mocking voice from the darkness. "You're breaking my heart, you are."

"Shhush, Dad," came a younger voice. "I want to hear the rest of it. It's good stuff."

"Ignore them, Uncle," urged Skeema. "Carry on."

Fearless did just that. "Let us pledge ourselves, dear kits, dear happy few, to give our all for this egg, weak mammals though we be. And if this brave stand proves to be our last, so be it! There's no small burrower or mighty Upworlder who, hearing of this deed, won't praise us for our pluck and wish they had been here to see it! *Together* is our watchword, Really Mads. We shall fight *together* to the last!"

"SKWEEE-SKWEEE!" came Snap-snap's death-defying cry once more.

Then, wonder of wonders, the sound found an echo in the air. "*SKWEEE-SKWEEE!*"

All heads went up towards it.

The voice from the air came again, this time with: "BOMBS AWAY!"

"AYEEE!" howled the leader of the Black-backs.

There was a sound of thundering feet, then a booming shout: "Good shot, Fledgie! You splatted that one right in his yellow eye! I'll take this next one."

There was a loud sound, not a thump exactly, but the satisfying *whack* of a three-toed foot connecting with a cowering backside. There were more such beautiful sounds to come as one by one the big bullies were boffed and booted. The attack was so surprising, so furious, so deadly accurate, that in three or four blinks of a gecko's eyelid, the whole pack of jackals was sent... well... *packing!*

Yi! Yi! Yi!

And every time they heard that flying foot making contact with an enemy's bottom, a cheer went up from the Really Mads – *"Hooray! Bravo!"* – because they all knew *exactly* the right word for the sound it made: *BIFF*.

Yes, it was *BIFF* to the rescue, just in the nick of time... *BIFF! BIFF! BIFF!*

Game over.

Chapter 9

After the battle, the feathered allies of our furry heroes were forced to take a breather. Fledgie had been nonstop on the wing for almost a suntime and a darktime. As soon as the Black-backs had fled, he dropped out of the sky, landed on the branch of a well-grazed fever tree and immediately drifted off to the land of drongo-dreams.

Biff had been on the run for just as long

(mostly in circles, as Uncle had guessed) when Fledgie had found him and led him in a straight headlong dash back to the nest.

All this and a lot of biffing had tired him out completely. His great chest pumped in and out like a giant bullfrog's throat. His head was spinning and his knees began to buckle. Suddenly he was towering over the Really Mads. As they stood together, still faithfully on guard and at their post, they looked up nervously. There he was, with one enormous scaly leg plonked firmly on either side of them. They saw his whacking, blue-grey thighs begin to shiver and shake high above them.

"Tim-berrrr!" cried Uncle. "He's coming down!" The kits took that as the order to

retreat… and
scattered. They
were not a moment
too soon! The giant
bird folded up
like a
concertina and
jolly nearly sat on the
lot of them. Even as
he collapsed, Biff's

ostrich-instinct led him to lay down his body to protect his last-remaining egg. With a sigh like a burst tyre, he closed the lids over eyes the size of tsamma melons and dozed peacefully.

"Phew!" breathed Uncle, dusting himself down. "Typical ostrich! Very sudden they are, you know, and bad-tempered with it. Not like me at all, what-what! Anyway, it looks as if the chickie's safe and sound again."

"Let's hope so," said Skeema doubtfully.

"Well, *I* shouldn't like to be under that lot!" said Mimi, looking at Biff's mountain of a body.

"Brrrr!" said Little Dream, yawning and shaking. "I'm freezing. What shall we do now, Uncle? It's going to be ages before suntime and Warm-up time. Shall we sniff around for a bolthole?"

"No need for that, Dreamie," said Fearless with a shiver. Now that the heat and excitement of the battle had died down, he himself was feeling the Upworld-cold. "We'll slip in here!" And very gently, so as not to disturb Biff, he lifted up the sleeping ostrich's wing. "Easy, now. Don't wake him," he whispered and, quiet as bats, he and the kits tucked themselves under it and at last they got some well-deserved rest themselves.

Not surprisingly, being so cosy under their unusual duvet, the meerkats were not exactly eager to crawl out into the chilly Upworld when the warm rays of the sun pushed at the darktime. Still, in this strange and dangerous place it was comforting to go through a regular warm-up routine.

Tiptoeing out of Biff's long shadow, Skeema, Mimi and Little Dream stood in line beside Uncle and had their usual scratch and stretch. In a trance, Uncle lowered his arms and placed his paws under his rather portly tummy. Absent-mindedly, he hoisted his tummy-pad towards the rising sun with a *"One-two-three… HUP!"*

This never failed to make the kits giggle. They thrust out pretend fat-tummies of their own and lifted them up all at once with a chorus of *"One-two-three… HUP!"* Then they had a special treat. Fledgie fluttered down from his roosting place to

join them with a drongo version of tummy-hoisting.

"It had to happen, I suppose," whispered Uncle with a mock-growl. "You've finally turned into a meerkat, Fledgie, you young rascal! Welcome to the Really Mads! Now get that jolly old tum-pad warmed up, and be quick and tricky about it! We need to start foraging and get some food inside us if we're going to build up our strength and our planning-muscles! We've got some big problems to solve, by all that's testing."

You don't get solar panels on a drongo's tummy, of course, but the ones on the rest of the Really Mads' tummies were working well that suntime. In a twinkling the kits were warmed up and scampering over to the base of the fever tree, where they dug away among its roots while Uncle kept a look-out. And what a Christmas-morning breakfast they had! This spot was alive with scorpions and millipedes – *deee-lish!* There were also plenty of colourful reptiles – a specially tender spade-snouted worm lizard for Mimi, a striped skink for Skeema, a spotted one for Little Dream. And when it was Uncle's turn to dig, in no time at all he uncovered one of his all-time favourites: a flap-neck chameleon.

Fledgie took special delight in the grubs and beetles that were thrown to him and when someone disturbed a nest of six-eyed sand-spiders, he thought he was back in drongo-dreamland. Gosh, those scuttlers were nippy! Fledgie had to dart all over the place to catch them.

And it was while he was flitting along, chasing one of the fattest of these leggy snacks, that he saw something dart out from a hole between some large rocks.

At once he knew it was the Black-backs' den.

He flew back as fast as he could to warn the Really Mads... and was rather surprised that Uncle didn't sound the alarm. "After the kicking they got from Biff," Uncle said, "my guess is that they've high-tailed out of this territory for a while. They'll be licking their wounds and trying their luck somewhere far, far away."

"Don't you think it would be wise to check?" asked Skeema.

"Impudence!" cried Uncle. "Do my job for me, would you? I know what's wise, what-what!"

"Sorry, Uncle," said Skeema, rolling on his back to show he meant it. "But I was rather hoping you'd let me go scouting with Fledgie and make sure the Black-backs aren't getting ready for another attack. We'll be ever so careful."

"I see. Harrrumph! Right. Apology accepted. Off you go, then – and mind you don't get caught," muttered Uncle, secretly pleased by his nephew's eagerness to keep one leap ahead of the enemy.

So Skeema and Fledgie made their way stealthily to the entrance hole and peered into the darkness. They strained their ears for any sound, but heard none. "Pooh, what a whiff!" whispered Skeema. "Now, what's the best way to check whether there's anybody in?"

"We'll give them a howl, matey," chirped Fledgie. "Watch my beak now and I'll show you how it's done. Ready?"

Skeema crouched, ready to run for his life at the first sign of trouble, and watched as Fledgie threw back his head and made a sound exactly like a jackal calling up his friends.

"Woooo-ee-ee-ee! Whee-ahhh!" he howled. "Go on, you try it, matey!"

Skeema lifted his chin, opened his throat and went for it. "*Wheee-uhhh, whip-whip!*"

They cocked their ears and waited, hearts pounding.

No reply. Nothing.

"Let's go for it, then," said Skeema. "You keep watch at the entrance here while I check out the den."

Down the well-trodden passageway he scampered, screwing up his face at the smell. He was expecting a long tunnel, but he realised as he began crunching on eggshells that after only a few steps he had reached the wide main chamber. It was not completely dark in here, and as his eyes grew accustomed to the gloom, he saw that there was no hope for Biff's chicks. The jackals must have gobbled the lot of them.

As he turned to leave, something glimmered beyond the shattered eggshells. He moved towards it, reaching for it with his paw. And then he knew. It was the little tin Vroom-vroom that he had last seen growing like fruit from the tree by the Ticktocks' burrow!

He scrabbled around and found, tucked into corners, heaps of the sparkling climbers and creepers (what we would call tinsel and silvery ribbons and a string of fairy lights) that they had seen dressing the Tick-tock family tree! Fledgie had told him about jackals being like crows that enjoy collecting anything shiny – and of course that is just what this stuff was!

He carried on searching and found a golden star covered with glass gems of many colours. More of the fruit from the tree turned up – a water pistol and a pair of binoculars and a wind-up radio… all sorts of shiny little things that Blah-blah cubs like to play with… Oh, and a dolly in a pink sparkly dress. Curled in one dark corner he found what he thought might be a snake. But when he grabbed it by the neck to shake the life out of it, it cried out: *jing-jing-jing-a-ling!* He dropped it, terrified, and sprang back, growling. He had never heard a sound like that... and yet... *Could* it be? Was it the sound that Uncle said he heard in this same season long ago? Hadn't he told a tall story about a fat Blah-blah in a red skin being dragged along by a donkey that went *jing-jing*?

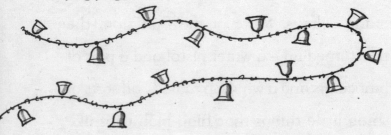

He dashed back out into the sunlit Upworld to tell Fledgie what he had discovered, and then they hurried off to show his treasures to the others.

So when Biff at last woke up, it was to the sound of Fledgie's excited *"Chip-chip! Chirro-kee-chirro-kee!"*

His big eyes flew open and his neck stretched out to see a fork-tailed drongo and a line of little meerkats gazing up at him with their arms full of strange, glittering things.

"BREAKFAST!" Biff boomed.

The Really Mads jumped back, thinking he might mean them, but he apparently had his eye on the fairy lights that Uncle was holding. Biff made a sudden grab for them and only let go because Fledgie managed to mimic the warbling trill of an ostrich chick.

That did the trick all right. Suddenly Biff was up and dancing, his great black and white wings spread. He stopped and peered closely at the egg he had been sitting on so long. It was still just lying there, warm and snugly wrapped in feathers. But the shell was unbroken and there wasn't a peep from inside it.

"Oh, BLOW!" boomed Biff, miserably disappointed and obviously in a temper. "BLAST AND BLITHER! I must have been hearing things! I was hoping he would hatch in the night. But look! He hasn't even started to break out! He's my only hope, the last of all my promising little ones." His proud neck drooped. "He's getting weaker all the time. He needs a mother!" he sighed. "But what am I going to do? All my wives were chased off by cheetahs! I shall never see any of them again."

"I say, look here!" said Uncle. "I think we might be able to help you there."

"YOU? How could a tiny little feller like you possibly help?" demanded Biff, pushing his enormous beak alarmingly close to Fearless.

"Sprintina!" announced Fearless, looking him right in the eye. "We know where she is. We could take you to her."

"Sprintina?" echoed Biff. "My favourite wife! I thought I'd lost her for ever! Where is she? Tell me! TELL ME!"

"East of here," said Little Dream softly, trying to calm him. "Did you notice that very bright star in the darktime? She's over that way."

"ARRRGH!" exclaimed Biff and lunged forward.

"Yikes!" squealed the kits and hopped out of the way like tree frogs. Only Uncle held his ground without so much as flinching. He watched Biff shovel up a huge beakful of pebbles. "Mmmya mmmmyooo mmmmeev mmmyegg!" he mumbled.

"I can't understand you if you talk with your mouth full," said Mimi, shocked and haughty.

It was rather foolish of her to take this attitude when she might easily be the next mouthful, but Biff apologised. "Quite right!" he agreed as he swallowed, everyone watching in horror as they saw the shape of the pebbles slide all the way down his

throat. "Manners. Forgive me. I'M UPSET! I have to take these for my digestion you know, and I haven't eaten properly for ages. I was trying to say that I'm in a mess. I don't know what to do. My chick won't hatch because he's pining for his mother and I miss her too. But we're here, and Sprintina's goodness knows where. Meanwhile our egg needs somebody sitting on it all the time. IT'S IMPOSSIBLE! It's hopeless."

"Excuse me," said Skeema. For a while

now he had been gazing at the powdery green bark of a bough from the fever tree with two empty bird's nests still clinging to it. It was lying in the sand nearby, having been torn down and left by some careless hungry elephant.

"What is it, laddie?" asked Uncle.

"A plan," answered Skeema. "I've just thought of one."

Chapter 10

The easy part of Skeema's plan was sorting out the nests. One was securely attached to the bough, but it needed a bit of mending and re-lining. Ostrich feathers did nicely for that. The other had to be tied comfortably on to Uncle's back. Fledgie was an excellent weaver and a quick worker and he showed the others how to help with twigs and feathers so that everything was tight and safe and cosy.

The hard part was lashing the bough to Biff's tail feathers.

He couldn't see the point of this at all, so Skeema had to explain it to him several times. "You're speedy!" he reminded Biff, without upsetting him by mentioning that he was only a little bit slower than a cheetah. "You said yourself that we have to get Chickie to its mother fast, right? But you can't carry the egg yourself. So this way, *we* can sit on it and keep it warm and safe, and *you* can run and pull us all to Sprintina!"

"And we can also take back all the shiny things that the jackals stole from the Ticktock cubs!" said Little Dream impatiently.

"They were so nice to Sprintina," said

Mimi. "She might not still be alive if they hadn't carried water to her."

"Oh, all right!" agreed Biff grudgingly. "But what if we meet an enemy? Tell me that! I shan't be able to outrun him if I'm dragging a branch behind me, you know!"

"Allow me to present you with a special anti-predator device…" said Skeema, looping something over Biff's head.

And so Biff set off towards the east, dragging behind him a most unusual sleigh and wearing round his neck a string of bells that went *jing-jing-jing-a-ling* all the way home. Uncle sat astride the main branch, carrying his nestful of shiny objects. Behind him, the kits formed themselves into a knot, gripping the egg and keeping it warm and hanging on for dear life with whatever spare paws and claws they could muster. If Biff was worried that he would soon get lost and start running in circles, he need not have been. Fledgie knew exactly where to go and he led the way. Sometimes he flew just in front of the ostrich and sometimes he took a short rest on his head.

Biff trotted on without stopping, past grazing herds of giraffe and gemsbok, red hartebeest and blue wildebeest that turned their heads in amazement to see the splendid plume of dust Biff raised as he ran. Zebra and dik-dik darted away in panic, thinking that Biff might be some new roarer they had never seen before.

On raced Biff, so keen to reach his goal that he narrowly missed a pride of lions guarding a cub. One moment they were all stretched out and yawning, the next, showing their teeth and growling ferociously.

"What do I do? What do I do?" cried Biff, rolling his eyes in terror.

"We're fine; trot on," called Fearless, who had broken off a springy twig to use as a whip and gave the lions a royal wave with it.

"It's the Three Beauties!" cried Little Dream. "And look – there's our friend Griff! Hello, Griff! Sorry, can't stop!"

"Just give 'em a jingle and giddy-hup!" urged Uncle, cracking the whip. "Don't worry, they won't bite you – they owe the kits a favour. I'll tell you a story, if you like, about how Skeema, Mimi and Little Dream once rescued that young cub. Well, it all began..."

But Biff, who had quickened his pace and was shaking the jingly bells like mad, never heard a word of Uncle's yarn.

They travelled so rapidly that when they caught sight of the white walls of the Tick-tocks' upside-down burrow, it was still Christmas morning. The Really Mads narrowed their eyes and peered through the choking red dust, clinging grimly to their precious gifts and trying to catch a glimpse of Sprintina. There was not a sign of her.

"Perhaps she's run off!" the kits whispered to one another. "Maybe she's gone the other way looking for Chickie!"

"I'm sure she's around here somewhere, matey!" chirped Fledgie. "But all I can see at the moment are sand dunes!"

"Whuh-where is she?" panted Biff. "Surely -huh!-she can't miss us-hah!-what with all this-heh!-jing-jing and dust!"

"Don't just jingle, matey; give a call!" suggested Fledgie.

"Can't!" gasped Biff. "I'm whacked. No breath left!"

"Leave it to me," said the little bird cheerily. He opened his throat and boomed out,

"Wooooo- ooooo- OOOOHoooooooo!"

At that, just three or four leopards' leaps in front of them, a pile of sand began to stir and rise! Back boomed a ghostly reply, not so loud and lusty, but definitely pleased-to-see-you. *WOOOO-hooooo!*

"Wup-wup!" cried Uncle for joy. "There she blows! A sandy-coloured sight for sore eyes! How about that for camouflage, eh, what? Whoa now, Biff! Whoa-up there!"

"Brilliant!" cried Skeema admiringly and

gave Snap-snap a "*SKWEEE*" to celebrate.

Biff was unhitched from the sand-sleigh in the flick of a lizard's tongue. He stood as still as an out-of-breath ostrich possibly can. Sprintina approached him shyly and silently, bobbing her neck. Nothing seemed to happen for a while. Everything froze. Then all at once Biff burst into bloom like a wonderful black and white flower! He puffed out his plumes and spread his wings wide to greet his lost love. Then down he went, kneeling before her, bowing very low, folding up his neck. She curtseyed and fluttered and twisted, and finally she spoke. "Is it really you, my brave Biff? I'd given you up for dead! We must dance!"

Biff suddenly stretched up to his full

height. "We'll dance later, my dear!" he boomed excitedly. "First, you need to SIT."

"B-but I've been lying here for I don't know how long," she said. "Why would I need to sit?"

"Because we have a present for you," said Biff. He turned to the kits, who remained at their post on the bird's nest, clinging together in a tight group-hug. As one, they jumped back and showed her what they were minding. And there it was – TA-DAHHHH! – the egg.

"I don't believe it! It couldn't be..." Sprintina crouched down to bring her beak level with the shell and gave it a tap. "Are you in there, my chickie?" she whispered. "Are you really alive? It's Mum here. Won't

you come out and see me?"

The ears of the Really Mads picked up a faint "*chee*" or "*peep*".

"What was that?" whispered Sprintina. "Are you cheeping to me, chickie? Are you?"

The "*chee-chee-chee*" became a tiny bit louder, just loud enough for all the Really Mads to hear, anyway. Then the egg gave a *tiny* little shiver. It wasn't much but Sprintina gave a hoot of pure joy, squatted and plonked herself firmly down on it. She gave a contented waggle to settle her feathers and fixed herself in the brooding position. She closed her eyes in order to give the egg her full attention. "Not much longer to wait now, Biff," she promised.

"Well done, everybody. Good show! Mission accomplished, I'd say."

"Not quite, Uncle," said Mimi. "The Tick-tock cubs. Remember?"

"Oh my goodness, yes! How forgetful of me. And here I am with the nest on my back and everything! Congratulations, Biff and Sprintina. And goodbye! Sorry to rush off, but we really must crack on. So, are you ready, Really Mads? Let's finish the job!"

"WHAT!" boomed Biff in a rage. "The fur-faced CHEEK of it! Of all the SAUCY, SHAMELESS, RUDE, IN-CONSIDERATE…"

"N-now, look here, old chap," stammered Uncle. "What has brought on this outburst?"

"Don't you 'old chap' me, you, you, you QUADRUPED!" raged Biff.

"B-but…"

Biff cut him off. "You and your MEASLY little mob cross an unknown stretch of the desert to find me!" he cried. "You protect my last surviving egg from a pack of stinking

NEST-ROBBERS! You come up with a brilliant plan to transport that egg, and you reunite me with my favourite wife when I thought I should never see her again! And now you intend to go off BY YOURSELVES to bring joy to the very Tick-tock cubs who brought life-saving water to Sprintina? DISGRACEFUL! Have you no thought for my HONOUR? How could you THINK of leaving without asking me to assist in some way?"

"Y-you mean, you want to come and help us?" asked Uncle, scratching his head in amazement. "But I thought you'd prefer to stay here with your wife and chickie!"

"But I don't intend to leave them for long, you MONGOOSE! Do you take me for some sort of BIRD BRAIN? Did you think I, a proud ostrich, would just stick my head in the sand and not do SOMETHING to pay back what I owe? Well, let me tell you something, mister. OSTRICHES DO NOT STICK THEIR HEADS IN THE SAND. Ooh, I'm so SICK of hearing that! Is that clear? Give me a job!"

"Very well, then," said Uncle firmly. "I understand why you're upset. There is something you can do, but—"

"What do you want me to do? Just TELL me!"

"I'm TRYING to tell you, by all that thunders!" cried Uncle, pulling himself up to his full twenty-six centimetres. "Calm down! Thank you. Now, you may help us, but only

on condition that you stop booming and follow my orders. Is that understood? We'll do this the meerkat way. Teamwork is the thing."

"Well, I—"

"Good. That's settled, then," said Uncle, cutting in firmly. "And now we must hurry, so you can make yourself useful by giving us a lift over to the Tick-tocks' territory."

"Aye-aye, captain," muttered Biff, hastily folding his enormously long legs backwards into the ostrich kneeling position. He turned to Sprintina, who was sitting pretty on her precious egg. "I shan't be long, dear," he said. "Keep your head down. Any problems, just boom."

The Really Mads clambered aboard Biff's broad back and they were off, watching Fledgie's forked tail streaming in the wind in front of them.

They reached the dreadful wire fence in

double-quick time. "Are the Tick-tocks on the other side of THIS?" demanded Biff. "I'll never get through there! What am I going to do – TUNNEL UNDER? Do you expect me to FLY over or something?"

"Harrumph!" said Uncle. "Stay put! Remember our bargain. Keep calm and wait for orders, what-what!"

"Quite right. Sorry. Over-excited," said Biff.

"He has got a point, though, Uncle!" said Little Dream.

Uncle's fur was sparking now. He felt quick and tricky and ready for anything. "Fledgie, when I say so, I want you to fly close to the Tick-tocks' burrow and mimic a polecat. But wait till I give you the signal. Dreamie, I need you with me. And here's what I want the rest of you to do..."

Chapter 11

"Kurra-kurra-kurra!"

At the sound of the polecat, all four Tick-tocks came running out of the house, shouting and waving their arms.

Immediately they froze in their tracks and slapped their hands over their mouths in amazement. They could not believe their eyes! When they looked through their wire fence and saw what was happening just a little way out into the desert, they thought at first they must be dreaming.

Was that really *a little sandman wearing a safari scarf and a bush hat? And could that really be an ostrich standing as still as... well... as a Christmas tree?*

Molly and Ajahn began to skip and dance for joy. Their astonished mama and papa tried to keep them back, but the little girl and boy had no fear. They ran through the gate and did not stop until they were up close to Biff, their eyes wide with wonder. How magnificent he looked, festooned with their very own fairy lights and tinsel. The lost presents were hanging from him too: the tin car, the water pistol, the wind-up radio, the binoculars – and the dolly in

the pink sparkly dress. Suddenly the little
girl was pointing and the little boy lifted his
gaze up and up, following the long neck
of the proud bird to the very top. And there
he was treated to
a sight that no
Blah-blah cub in
the whole of the
Kalahari had ever
seen before. It was
the special golden
star all covered with
glass gems of many
colours, held up over
the ostrich-tree's head
by Mimi, the meerkat
princess!

A movement in the sand nearby suddenly drew all eyes to something that, because of all the excitement, hadn't caught their attention before. A sandy-coloured female ostrich had been sitting quite still and now, without warning, she leapt to her feet. And lying in the sand for all eyes to see was the single, precious egg that she had been sitting on.

It gave a jolt and a judder. Then it started to rock slightly and a little piece of shell jumped away from the side of it like a bit of broken china. All the onlookers could see a bluish, transparent membrane stretched across the hole, a small window on to the Upworld lit by the Kalahari Christmas sun. The window was pushed and poked from the inside by a tiny beak and – pop – *there was the head*! A struggle. *"There's a wing, look!"* A nudge, a last heave, a slippery dive... and there he was – the best Christmas present that Biff and Sprintina could ever have wished for!

All the tongues of the Blah-blahs who saw him, ticked and tocked a welcome and even the sheep and the chickens darted out to admire the newborn chickie.

"Hooray! Happy hatchday!" called Mimi as she slid down Biff's neck for a closer look. She put the star she'd been holding into the arms of their mini sand-Blah-blah and ran to join the crowd admiring the funny little mottled grey blob on stilts.

"Well, here he is at last, by all that's brave and damp and tottering!" muttered Uncle, bursting with pride and secretly brushing away a tear of relief as Biff, the proud father wearing all his Christmas finery, started teaching his newborn chickie how to pick

up bits of gravel. "Call me a big old softie, but isn't this season wonderful? Aren't babies wonderful?"

Then all of a sudden Fearless let out a shout and sprang high into the air as if sharp teeth had just fastened on his tail. "Oh my goodness! Babies! My babies! Defenceless, without their royal father to protect them! Wup-wup! Gather to me at the double, Really Mads!" he cried.

"Wait," begged Mimi. "The little Blah-blahs have got something for us."

And indeed, Molly and Ajahn were kneeling in the sand. Molly had unwound three strings of beautifully coloured beads – her *amandavathi* – from her ankles, and she was holding them out in front of her.

"Take them," said Uncle. "They're a mark of respect." And one by one the little girl placed them round the necks of Mimi, Skeema and Little Dream.

"The small male has something for you," said Little Dream, turning to Uncle.

"Harrumph. Well... naturally!" said Fearless, who had secretly feared for a moment that he might be left out. He stood bravely in front of the little boy and lifted his noble chin. Ajahn reached down and popped a handful of grubs into his mouth. At the same time, he attached to the royal radio-collar a fabulous beaded ornament in the shape of a Christmas tree.

Uncle let out a bubbling call that was both a shout of pleasure and also meant, "Goodbye, everyone, and good luck! Tally ho!"

Then, much to the *stonishment* of the awe-struck ostriches, the sheep, the chickens and the Tick-tocks – not to mention a newly hatched chickie – the marvellous meerkat mob gathered together in a tight bunch, waving their tails together like elegant grasses bending in the wind, as they danced a Meerkat Farewell.

And then, like a melted dream, like a puff of wind – they were gone.

*

"Poor old Uncle!" puffed Skeema as they galloped closer and closer to the burrow.

"He's bound to get it in the neck from Radiant!"

"And in the tail," added Mimi. "We've all been gone for ages! She'll be worried sick!"

"Call this a jiffy, you wicked old thing?" came the indignant voice of Radiant from above their heads. "Where were you in the darktime when we needed you?" Fledgie couldn't resist finishing off with a – "*tweety tweet tweet!*" – or they would never have guessed it was him doing the scolding.

"Fledgie, will you stop that mimicking and mickey-taking, by all that echoes!" wailed Uncle. "As if I haven't had enough to worry about lately! Hurry, everyone! Hurry!"

"We'll all be in trouble," panted Little

Dream. "And what will Mama say?"

They skidded to a halt in a cloud of dry dust, no more than a springbok's pronk from the burrow-entrance and they saw... not a wink, not a whisker of a meerkat mob!

"Oh, no!" cried Uncle. "The place is deserted! Something dreadful must have happened to them! An enemy mob, perhaps! A pack of hyenas!"

Just then, a mischievous little nose followed by a saucy pair of ears and eyes popped out of a nearby bolthole. "Naughty Daddy!" squeaked Trouble, for it was he. "Nip-nip for you!"

Fearless let out a gasp of relief, gathering the teeny-tiny kit in his arms, giving him a cuddle and a squeeze. "Where's your mama, dear old chap?" he cooed. "Where are your brothers and sisters?"

"Peepo!" squeaked Zora the Snorer, Quickpaws and Bundle, pinging out of boltholes like pips from a wild cucumber.

And no sooner had Fearless rolled the delighted babies all about and given them all a jolly good squirt than their mother appeared.

At once, Fearless began to bob and duck and make excuses. "I say! Now, look here, dear-heart! I know exactly what you must be thinking. But, harrumph, just give me a chance to explain. You see, I didn't mean to be absent for so long, only there was a bit of an emergency. A thieving bunch of Black-backs robbed the Tick-tocks, d'you follow me? Well, we couldn't just stand by and do nothing, could we? Had to get on their trail, track the blighters across unknown territory. That got us into some shocking scrapes. Why, we had to…"

The kits began to chip in eagerly, all talking at once:

"… dodge a charging square-lipped rhino and her giant baby!"

"…help a lost ostrich to find his mate!"

"…and rescue their very last chickie!"

"…have a huge big battle with the jackals!"

"… and grab back the shiny treasure they stole!"

"… and bring everything back to where the Tick-tocks live."

Radiant put her arms round Fearless and gave him – not a nip, not a telling-off but only a long and loving lick. "As long as you all enjoyed yourselves, you and these young scallywags!" she said cheerfully. "How could I be cross? Especially," she went on, admiring the beaded ornament that dangled from Fearless's collar, "when you've brought back something nice for Fragrant's

newborns to chew on!"

"Newborns?" yelled the kits.

"You mean we've got more brothers and sisters?" squealed Dreamie. "Whee!"

"Well, strictly speaking, they're your half-brothers and sisters," said Radiant. "But this isn't the season for strictness, is it now, my lovelies?"

"Please can we see them?" begged Mimi. "Can we see Mama and the new babies? Pleeeeease!"

"You'd better have a word with the proud father, my dear," said Radiant. "Here he comes now, if I'm not mistaken."

And indeed, right on cue, Broad Shoulders appeared, heaving his powerful body out of the burrow entrance. He was looking weary – but mighty pleased with himself. "I'm a papa! Mission accomplished!" he announced, proud as a peacock. "How about you chaps?"

"Well," declared Fearless. "Without wishing to boast or anything, I think we can say the same, what-what!" chuckled Uncle. "Am I right, my Really Mad warriors?"

"Hear, hear! Mission accomplished!" cheered the kits.

"Then off you go and introduce yourselves to four little strangers!" said Broad Shoulders.

Down the tunnel raced the kits, each determined to be the first to catch a glimpse of their dear mama, Fragrant, nursing her newborn babies.

And as the meerkats greeted one another

and rejoiced, Fledgie Drongo, H.M. (Honorary Meerkat) flew loop-the-loops in the skies above them, in celebration of this marvellous and quite *stonishing* Kalahari Christmas.

THE END

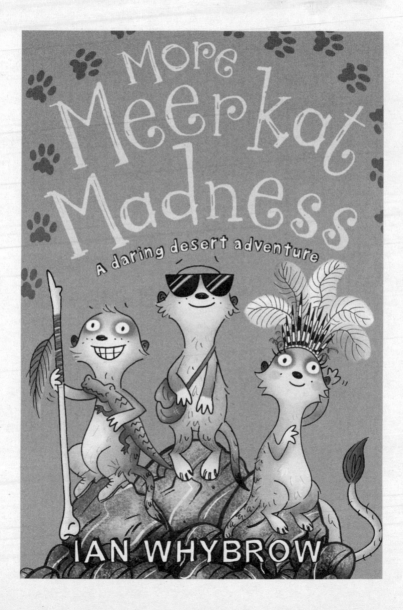

Have you read…?

Awesome Animals

Watch out for the world's wildest pandas!

PANDA PANIC

Jamie Rix